IMAGINE THAT

Licensed exclusively to Imagine That Publishing Ltd
Tide Mill Way, Woodbridge, Suffolk, IP12 1AP, UK
www.imaginethat.com
Copyright © 2019 Imagine That Group Ltd
All rights reserved
2 4 6 8 9 7 5 3 1
Manufactured in China

Written by Dan Crisp
Illustrated by Mark Chambers

ISBN 978-1-84956-302-4

A catalogue record for this book is available from the British Library

PANDAMONIUM

Written by Dan Crisp   Illustrated by Mark Chambers

For Mum, Dad and Caleb Crisp - Dan

For Lucinda, who smells great! - M.C

As the zookeeper snored,
The great lion roared,

ROOAAR!

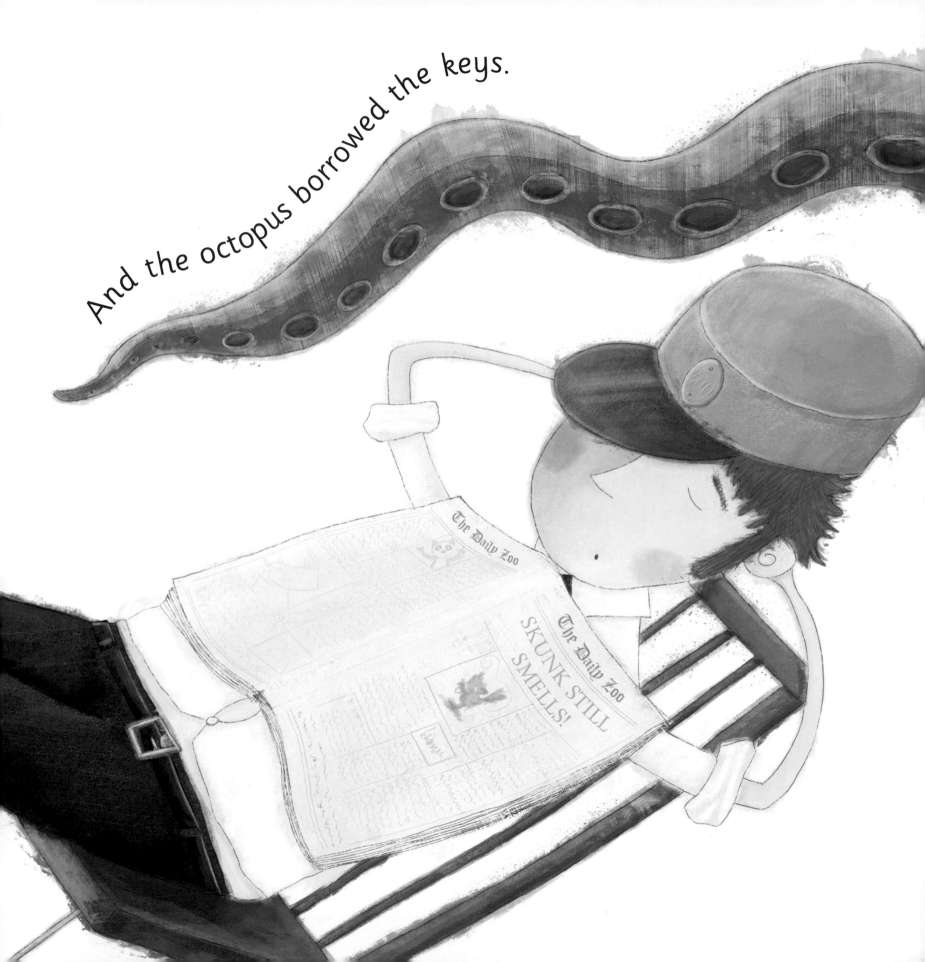

And the octopus borrowed the keys.

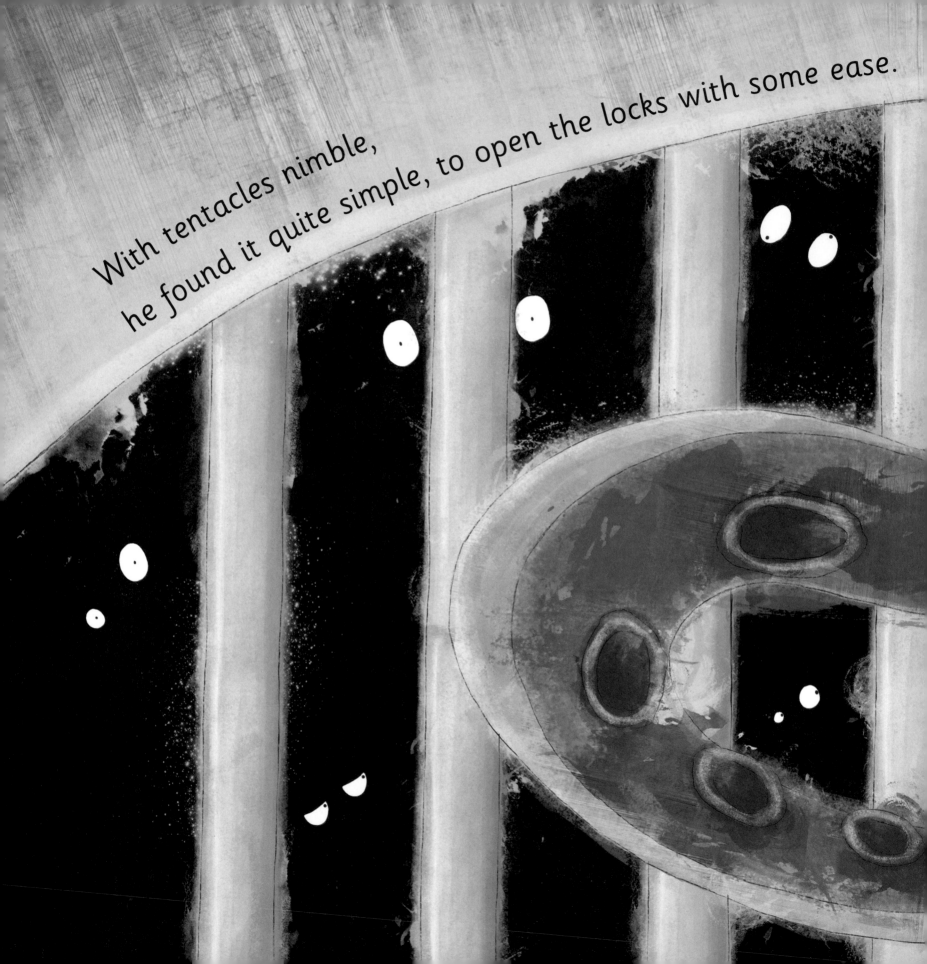

With tentacles nimble, he found it quite simple, to open the locks with some ease.

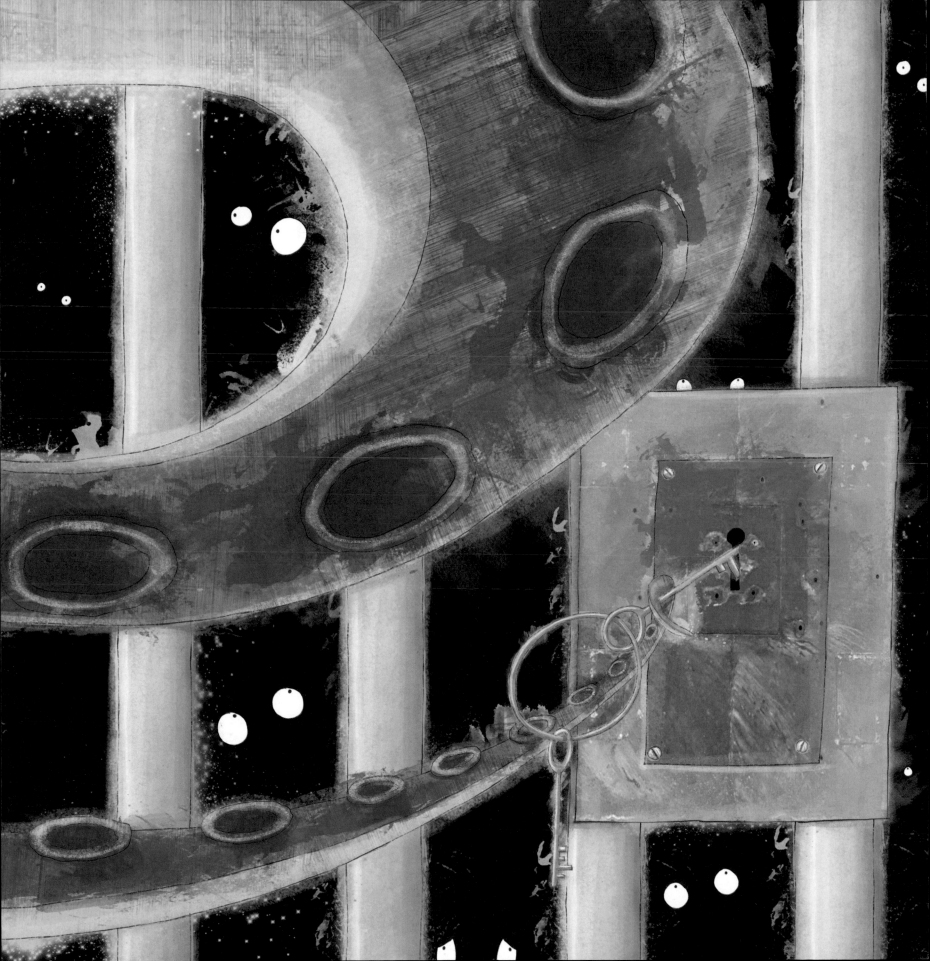

When all the animals were freed,
The pandas agreed,

That the party
should really begin.

The flamingos' excitement,

PARTY!

At the pandas' announcement,

Caused the hyenas to grin.

A change in the mood!
PANDAmonium ensued!

Rousing even
the dodo from sleep.

A party all round!
And despite all
the sound,

From the zookeeper;
still not a peep.

But just then the skunk,
(who was dressed as a punk)

Nasty pong

↓

Did such an unsavoury thing.

'Now, who's made that stink?'
Said the polecat to the mink,
As their eyes were beginning to sting.

'Back to your cages!
That pong will stay for ages!'

Squealed the elephant, knotting his trunk.

On detecting the smell,
The turtle put his head in his shell,

And the monkey jumped back in his bunk.

Monkeys Only

But then the zookeeper's nose,
And the tips of his toes,

Suddenly started to twitch.

Twitchy nose

He pricked up his ears,
And his eyes filled with tears,
At the odour that was so very rich.

He woke from his dreams,
Said, 'I'm giving up beans!'

And returned to
reading his paper.